marty mcguire

digs worms!

marty mcguire
digs worms!

BY Kate Messner

ILLUSTRATED BY Brian Floca

SCHOLASTIC PRESS / NEW YORK

Library of Congress Cataloging-in-Publication Data

Messner, Kate.

Marty McGuire digs worms! / by Kate Messner ; illustrated by Brian

Floca. — 1st ed. p. cm.

Summary: With help from her Grandma Barb, Marty builds a habitat for

worms in her school cafeteria as part of the Save the Earth Project.

[1. Schools—Fiction. 2. Grandmothers—Fiction. 3. Environmental

protection—Fiction. 4. Recycling (Waste)—Fiction.

5. Worms—Fiction.] I. Floca, Brian, ill. II. Title.

PZ7.M5615Md 2012 [Fic]—dc23   2011016291

ISBN 978-0-545-14245-8

10 9 8 7 6 5 4 3 2 1   12 13 14 15 16

Printed in the U.S.A.   23

First edition, April 2012

For Barbara Napper and
Barbara Copeland Perry,
two science teachers who aren't afraid
of getting their hands dirty
—K.M.

For Lars, Andrea, and Ethan
—B.F.

chapter 1

As soon as I see the blackboard in my classroom Monday morning, I can tell it is going to be an extra-super week. There are three terrific things on Mrs. Aloi's "Third-Grade Stars Today" list.

1. Today is Monday!

Mondays are the best because we have library, and if you tell Ms. Stephanie about the last book you read, she gives you a Starburst from her secret stash under the librarian desk. Plus, Monday is veggie goulash day in the cafeteria, which would be awful except that they serve ice-cream cups for dessert because who would buy goulash if you weren't getting ice cream with it? So, Mondays are very tasty days.

2. Classroom helper this week is Marty McGuire!

I love being classroom helper because you don't have to sit still so much. You get to hand out papers and pick up papers and be line leader and take the lunch count down to the cafeteria all by yourself or with a friend. I'm going to ask my best friend, Annie, to go with me. Plus, you get to feed Horace, our class lizard. You have to remember to put the lid back on the jar of crickets when you're done or they get out and hop down the hall and scare Miss Gail, the art teacher.

3. We will have a special assembly before lunch!

When we have an assembly, we get to go to the auditorium with everyone in the whole school and sit in the springy chairs where the bottom

folds up and shuts you right up inside if you're not careful. I haven't been crocodile-snapped like that since kindergarten. At assemblies, an Interesting Person comes and talks instead of teachers. One time, the Interesting Person brought pythons and told us all about where pythons live and what they eat. One time, the Interesting Person brought costumes from a long time ago and let us try them on. And one time, three Interesting People came and rode unicycles right across the stage and didn't crash into one another even once. I wonder who it will be today.

The fourth thing on the "Third-Grade Stars Today" list is not so terrific.

4. First job today: math work sheet!

How exactly does a math work sheet deserve an exclamation point?

🐛

"Mrs. Aloi?" Veronica Grace Smithers says. "What's the assembly going to be about? There aren't going to be snakes again, are there?" Veronica Grace doesn't like anything that slithers or crawls.

"No, Veronica Grace. Not today."

"Awwww," says Rupert Wingfield. I look over at him and grin. I liked the Snake Lady, too.

"I hope we get somebody good," says Jimmy Lawson. "I hope it's that guy from the TV show where they drop him off in the wilderness and he has to survive. He could come in and eat bugs like he did on TV."

"Ewww!" says Veronica Grace.

"Hey!" Alex Farley jumps out of his seat and knocks his tool belt against his desk. "Maybe it'll be Mick Buzzsaw from *Handyman America*! He can build a swing-set right up onstage like he did on his show."

"Maybe it'll be somebody from the Nature Channel," says Annie.

"Maybe it'll be Lola Smitterly from *Dance-o-Rama*!" says Kimmy Butler.

"Oooh!" Veronica Grace says. "Maybe she'll bring cameras and put us on TV!"

Mrs. Aloi shakes her maracas. She does that to quiet us down. "It's time for us to go to the auditorium now. The guest for our assembly is a very special visitor who's here to talk with us about keeping the earth healthy. Line up, and remember to set a good example for the kindergartners."

I lead the class to the auditorium and go all the way down to the end of the front row like I'm supposed to. I keep both feet on the floor, and I don't twist around in my seat. I watch the first and second graders and kindergartners arrive. I wonder if our assembly person will be worth that exclamation point.

Only one kindergartner gets crocodile-snapped into her seat. As soon as her teacher lifts her out, our principal, Mrs. Grimes, goes up onstage in her clickety-clackety shoes. If those were my shoes up there, I'd jump around and make some more noise on that nice wood floor, but I guess Mrs. Grimes has very good self-control and that's why she gets to be principal.

"Welcome, students. It is my pleasure to introduce today's visitor to Orchard Street Elementary

School — a woman who has devoted her life to keeping our planet green. Ms. Amelia Ranidae!"

Amelia Ranidae steps onto the stage quietly — no clickety-clackety shoes for her. She's wearing hiking boots like Jane Goodall, and she's carrying an aquarium full of plants. When I look

closer, I see bright spots mixed in with the green leaves — red and yellow and even a blue one. The yellow spot jumps out of its plant and into the water dish.

It makes me jump, too, and Amelia Ranidae smiles. "Have you ever seen a poison dart frog from the Amazon rain forest?"

I shake my head no. Behind me, Rupert forgets to be auditorium-quiet and lets out a big "Whoooa!! Awesome!!"

He's right. Amelia Ranidae and her poison dart frogs deserve a whole page of exclamation points.

chapter 2

"You can call me the Frog Lady," says Amelia Ranidae. We were going to end up calling her that anyway. We still call that other Interesting Person the Snake Lady, and she didn't even give us permission.

"I want to introduce you to my friends. These frogs are beautiful to look at, but you have to be extra careful if you need to handle them, because they give off a kind of poison from their skin. They get their name — poison dart frog — from the indigenous people of South America. 'Indigenous' means the people who have always lived there. They use that poison on the tips of their darts and blowguns."

"Oh." Jimmy Lawson sounds disappointed. "I wanted to see the frogs shoot poison darts."

"Sorry," says the Frog Lady. "That would have been cool. But the frogs do use their poison as a defense. It convinces most predators to leave them alone."

"If you touched one of them, would you die?" asks Rupert.

"No," says the Frog Lady. "These frogs aren't as poisonous because they weren't born in the wild."

"How about if you ate your sandwich without washing your hands after you touched it?" asks Jimmy Lawson.

"Probably not," says the Frog Lady. "But you might get sick."

"How about if you ate the whole frog?" asks Jimmy. "Then would you die?"

"Ew!" says Veronica Grace.

Mrs. Aloi looks around. I bet she's wishing her maracas weren't back in the classroom.

"Okay," the Frog Lady says. "The most important thing I wanted to tell you about these interesting, beautiful frogs is that they're in danger because their habitat is being threatened. Does anyone know why?"

Annie raises her hand. "Is it because of people cutting down the rain forest? That's what's happening with the chimpanzees and mountain gorillas in Africa."

Annie and I know all about chimpanzees and mountain gorillas because of Jane Goodall and Dian Fossey, these awesome scientists who went to Africa to try to save them. Sometimes, we pretend to be Jane and Dian in the woods behind Annie's house. We pretend the crayfish are chimpanzees and mountain gorillas, even though they're not as cute.

The Frog Lady nods at Annie. "That's exactly right. These frogs are losing their habitat."

I look at the poor frogs on their leaves in the aquarium. It makes me want to go right to South America and take away all the equipment and stuff that they're using to chop down trees.

And just like she read my thoughts, the Frog Lady says, "So we're going to do something to help."

"Are we going on a field trip?" asks Rupert.

"Are we going to South America?" asks Jimmy Lawson.

"Awesome!" says Alex Farley.

"Do we have to take a plane?" asks Kimmy Butler.

mushy and then lifting up a screen underneath and that turned the mushy bits into new paper somehow."

Annie reaches down to put her socks back on. "Well, that doesn't sound hard. Want to start after dinner? I'll bring a bunch of paper from my house."

"Great." I tie my sneakers and jump down from my boulder. "And my dad just took the screens out of our windows to clean them. We can use one of those."

"Yay!" Annie does a happy, earth-saving jump. "Let's head home for dinner, and I'll meet you after."

I nod. "But let's patrol one last time, just in case."

We do. There are still no guys with axes. At least not that we can see.

They're sneaky sometimes, but we'll be ready for them.

chapter 4

When I get home, Dad is standing on the porch, waiting for Mom. "She should be home by now," he says. "Grandma's coming over for dinner."

"Which grandma?" I ask.

"Grandma Barb," Dad says.

"Oh, good." Grandma Barb is the cool one. She's my mom's mother and lives in a big old house and has a huge garden with rabbits. She yells at them when they eat her lettuce, but she likes them too much to do anything about it. When I visit Grandma Barb for a sleepover, we eat raw vegetables from the garden for dinner and make our own ice cream, and then late at night she gets me out of bed in my pajamas if the fireflies are out, and we catch them in jars to make lanterns. Then we let them go because it probably isn't much fun to be stuck in a lantern after a while.

Dad's mom, Grandma Joyce, is the boring one, but I'm not supposed to say so because that might hurt her feelings. Grandma Joyce likes to have tea when she comes to visit and wants me to sit with her and do quiet indoor things. She buys me princess paper dolls with stiff, fancy outfits for my birthday every year. I have them all in a box in my closet because I don't do paper dolls, especially not ones dressed in scratchy-looking dresses.

Finally, Mom's car pulls into the driveway and she gets out. There's a big thick bandage wrapped all around her arm. "Don't ask," she says, which means she has had a crazy bad day helping some animal that didn't want to be helped. Mom is a wildlife rehabilitator, so people call her when they find an animal that's sick or hurt. The trouble is, hurt animals can be pretty grumpy, and sometimes they have sharp claws and teeth and don't understand that Mom is on their side.

"Another raccoon?" Dad asks.

"Nope." Mom lifts the big back door of her station wagon and pulls out a cage full of feathers. I run up to her and look inside. A huge owl stares out at me with yellowy eyes. Really, really mad-looking yellowy eyes.

"Careful," Mom says. "Keep your fingers away from his cage."

I'm keeping my fingers and everything else away from that thing. His beak is all sharp and

hooked, and his talons are curved and pointy and fierce. He keeps staring and scowling at me like I'm the reason he's in that little cage, even though I just met him.

"What's wrong with him?" I ask. "He looks pretty healthy to me."

"His right wing is injured," Mom says. "He flew into a window on one of those big new houses up on Jacob's Hill."

Jacob's Hill used to be all woods, and we'd go there in winter to look for animal tracks until somebody bought the land and cut down the trees and built big houses all over. Annie and I weren't patrolling back then.

"Rachel," Dad says, looking at Mom's dirty hands and owl-rumpled clothes. "Did you remember your mom's coming for dinner?"

"No. I mean, yes, I remember, but I didn't have time to start dinner, obviously. Can you help with this?" She holds the cage out toward Dad, who looks like he wants nothing to do with an owl that might want to have him for dinner.

Grandma Barb shows up in her orange pickup truck then, and she solves everything. Grandma Barb is like that.

"Well, look at what we have here!" She hops out of the truck, takes off her sweater, and helps Mom move the owl to the back porch. Then she goes back to the truck and pulls out two big flat boxes.

"You brought pizza!" I run up and hug her.

"I called earlier, and nobody was home." Grandma Barb winks at Mom. "So I figured the chef might be otherwise occupied."

Dad gives Grandma Barb a hug. I'm not sure if he's happier about the pizza or being saved from the angry owl.

"I have to eat fast," I say when we sit down. "Annie and I are working on a school project after dinner. We have to save the earth."

"That's a pretty tall order," Grandma Barb says, taking a bite of her veggie pizza.

"No, it's okay," I tell her. "The rest of the class is helping, too."

"What's your project?" Dad asks.

I shake my head. "Top secret," I say. I want to surprise them with our paper when we're done.

Just as I'm finishing my second slice of pizza, Annie comes to the door with her arms full of old newspapers and magazines. "My mom gave me these to start with."

"Shhh!" I hustle her down to the basement.

I grab one of the window screens Dad left leaning against the stairs. Then I empty the soup cans out of our recycling bin, fill it with water in the basement sink, and drag it over next to Annie's pile of paper. "First we have to tear this up in tiny pieces," I say.

So we start ripping off little pieces and putting them into the water. After half an hour, Annie leans over to look in the recycling bin. "It still doesn't look like much."

"It should be starting to look like new paper," I say. But it doesn't. There are half sentences floating all over the bin. It definitely still looks like old, torn-up newspapers.

"Maybe you need to use different kinds of paper," Annie says. "Do you have any other paper stuff you don't want?"

I snap my fingers because I know where I can get a whole bunch of junky paper. "Be right back!"

"You don't want these?" Annie says when I get back. She flips through *Princess Paper Dolls of France*, *Princess Paper Dolls of Great Britain*, and *Princess Paper Dolls of the Middle East*.

"Nope." I punch out the Princess Margaret doll, rip her head off, and toss the pieces in the water. Annie does the same thing with Princess Grace, Princess Marie, Princess Elizabeth, and Princess Alia.

Now there are princess parts floating all

around with the newspaper bits. It still doesn't look like paper.

"Maybe the pieces aren't small enough," Annie says.

"Maybe not," I say. But I'm tired of ripping. "I know what we can do! When my dad makes salsa, he puts tomatoes and onions and everything into the food processor and it comes out in tiny little salsa pieces."

Annie looks a little worried. "Do you think it'll work with paper?"

"Why not?"

I tiptoe upstairs because I am a top-secret earth saver. Plus, if I ask to use the food processor, they'll probably say no.

Luckily, Mom and Grandma Barb have gone out to have coffee on the porch, and Dad is in the living room, watching the Red Sox on TV. The top-secret, earth-saving equipment is unguarded on the kitchen counter.

I carry it downstairs and plug it in. "Okay, start putting in paper."

"You want the wet paper or the dry paper?"

"Try some of both." I start scooping out handfuls of princess heads and newspaper ads while Annie tears off more bits of dry paper from a cooking magazine.

"Okay, that's good," I say. "Stand back."

I look for the ON switch, but it turns out there are a whole bunch of choices. "Hey, Annie? Do you think our paper ought to be sliced, chopped, shredded, or minced?"

Annie studies the switch. "Try slicing first."

I flip the switch to SLICE, and the thing starts whirring all around. Annie and I get down on our bellies so we can watch through the clear plastic, but we really can't tell if it's working because everything in there is zipping around too fast.

"Let's check it now!" Annie shouts over the

motor, so I turn it off and remove the lid. The newspaper bits look like they're in smaller pieces, but the princess heads are still whole.

"They're made of way thicker paper," Annie says. "Does chopping make that thing go faster? Try chopping them instead."

"Let's put more in, too." I quick rip up Princess Gabriella, push her down into the soggy news-paper bits, and put the lid back on top. When I flip the switch to CHOP, it gets even louder.

"Should I try shredding them?" I shout over

the motor. Annie nods, and I kick it up another notch so it's whining even louder. There's a little clicking noise every once in a while, like maybe it's finally working on the thicker paper.

"I think it's starting to work!" Annie yells. "Try MINCE now!"

I push the switch all the way over, and the motor gets even louder. The clicking's louder, too, and it's starting to turn into sort of a clunking once in a while. "Do you think we should check?!" I yell.

"Not yet!" Annie shouts. "I think we should wait a couple more —"

The food processor makes a crazy loud *THUNK* and stops.

I flip the switch on and off, but nothing happens.

Then there's a new sound. Not as loud as the crazy loud thunk but even scarier. Dad's footsteps coming down the basement stairs.

chapter 5

Dad stops on the bottom step. He looks at the soggy paper in the recycling bin. He looks at his food processor. He looks at me. "Marty, what are you doing?"

"Saving the earth?"

"With my food processor?"

I nod.

Dad walks over and pulls off the lid. Princess Grace's head is wedged under the blades. She smiles up at us, even though there's mushy news-paper in her hair.

Dad replaces the lid and presses the CHOP switch. Nothing happens. I look at my sneakers and whisper, "Sorry."

"Whatever possessed you to try and blend Grandma Joyce's paper dolls?"

"We weren't blending them," I say. "We were slicing them up to make recycled paper. Only they weren't slicing very well, so we tried to chop them and shred them and then mince them and that's where we got into trouble."

Dad pulls a princess arm out of the newspaper mush. "You're going to be saving your allowance for a long time to buy a new food processor." I nod. He unplugs it and heads back upstairs.

"Hmm," Annie says. "That didn't go so well."

"No." I stir the rest of the paper doll heads around the recycling bin with my hand.

"I hear someone's whipping up paper-doll-princess surprise for dessert!" Grandma Barb calls from the stairs. She walks over to us and peers into the bin of princess-head soup. "I think I'll pass. I'm kind of full."

"We broke Dad's food processor," I say.

"I heard."

"We were trying to make recycled paper for a

school project. We have to do something to help save the earth," Annie tells her.

"Making paper is pretty complicated," Grandma Barb says. She starts scooping handfuls of paper mush into the garbage can. When there's mostly gray water left, she lifts the bin and pours it down the sink. "What about a recycling project for your school cafeteria instead?"

"We already do that," Annie says. "We have bins like these for our plastic water bottles and fruit cups and things."

"What about the food?" Grandma Barb asks.

"We eat the food," I say. "Except the peas. We scrape those into the garbage."

"That's it!" Grandma Barb claps her hands so loud and fast that Annie and I both jump. When Grandma Barb gets an idea, you better watch out. "You need to recycle those peas!"

"Who would want used peas?"

"I know someone who would *love* your used peas." Grandma Barb grins and stands up. "Ask your mom if you can come to my house after school tomorrow."

chapter 6

When Grandma Barb picks us up from school, she doesn't even wait for us to put our backpacks in the house. "Follow me!" She jumps out of her truck and goes straight to the back of her house where she keeps her compost bin.

When we have dinner at Grandma Barb's house, I always take the vegetable peels out and put them in the pile, and after a long time, Grandma Barb says the bugs and bacteria and everything make them into compost that she can use to feed her garden. Are the bugs going to eat our peas?

But Grandma Barb hustles right past the compost bin to a long wooden bench that wasn't here last time I visited. "Here we are!" She waves her arm toward the bench. "I want you to meet my new friends."

Only there's nobody there.

Annie looks at me, and I can tell she's thinking my Grandma Barb is crazy, introducing us to her imaginary friends sitting on her new bench and thinking they might want our leftover peas.

But then Grandma Barb reaches down and lifts up the seat of the bench, and it turns out there's a secret compartment under there, all filled with dirt. "Hello, boys!" she says, and wiggles her fingers down into the soil. When she scoops up a handful, there are little red worms wiggling all through her fingers.

"Wow!" I say. "You have worms living in your bench!"

"They work for me," Grandma Barb says. "I give them a place to stay and all their food . . ." She digs down into the dirt and pulls up a cucumber peel that looks half eaten. ". . . and they turn it into black gold for my garden." She reaches behind the bench and pulls out a recycling bin like the one we tried to use for our paper project. It's full of dark, dark soil.

"They turn cucumber peels into dirt?" Annie pokes at the soil.

"That's not dirt. It's worm poop!"

Annie pulls her hand back, and Grandma Barb laughs.

I step in closer. "It looks like dirt," I say.

"It does, but it's really worm castings. That's the official name because most grown-ups don't like calling it worm poop. Worm castings are loaded with nutrients and stuff your garden needs to grow. It's the best fertilizer around."

"And you think your worms might want to eat our cafeteria peas, too?" I reach in and pull out a handful of dirt and worms. It tickles when they wiggle through my fingers.

"We can set up a couple benches just like this one in your school cafeteria if your principal says it's okay," Grandma Barb says. "I'd be happy to help you get started."

"Wow!" Annie says.

But then I think about our principal, Mrs. Grimes, in her nice, clean school dresses and clickety-clackety shoes. "I'm not sure our principal will like that."

"I'll come talk to her," Grandma Barb says.

And I smile. Now I know we'll get to do our project. Because once Grandma Barb gets an idea, you better watch out.

chapter 7

The next day, everyone in the class gets to share how they're going to help save the earth. Veronica Grace and Kimmy and Isabel are going to grow petunias from seeds so we can have flowers in a window box in our classroom.

"Lovely," Mrs. Aloi says. "And how will that help save the earth?"

Veronica Grace's forehead wrinkles like she forgot about that part. "Because they're pretty?"

"Well, yes," Mrs. Aloi says, "but you're really helping out in a different way. Plants give off oxygen that we breathe, and they help get carbon dioxide out of the air so it doesn't contribute to global warming."

Veronica Grace nods. "And they're pretty, too."

Rasheena's going to find a way to get her dad to stop throwing out things that can be recycled. "If I find cans in the garbage," she says, "I'm going to take them out and shove them under his pillow."

"Maybe there's a better way to remind him," Mrs. Aloi says. "We'll talk later."

Rupert Wingfield and Alex Farley share their idea next.

"How many of you have cans and bottles and old parts of broken things in your garages?" Rupert asks.

Every hand goes up.

"I'd like you to bring all that stuff to school tomorrow."

Mrs. Aloi's eyebrows shoot up so fast I think they're going to fly right off her forehead.

"Don't worry," Alex tells her. "We're going to recycle them."

Mrs. Aloi looks at the clock. "It's almost time for art class. Who still has to share?"

Annie and I wave our hands. We've been dying to share our project, ever since Grandma came to visit at lunch and said she got us permission to start our cafeteria worm farm. I guess Mrs. Grimes was a little worried at first, but Grandma promised her the worms don't get out and crawl

around, not even at night when no one's watching, so Mrs. Grimes said it was okay. "We're going to reduce the amount of garbage in the cafeteria," I say. Mrs. Aloi smiles.

"Wonderful," she says.

Annie nods. "Marty's grandma — the cool one, not the boring one — is going to come in and build a wooden bench in the cafeteria."

"How lovely!"

Annie nods. "Only it's not just a bench. When you lift the lid, there are thousands and thousands of worms inside, squirming all over the place. And they live there. And we'll put our peas and other gross stuff that nobody eats in the worm bench, and they'll eat our garbage and then we'll have lots of worm poop for fertilizer." Annie smiles at Mrs. Aloi.

"We can call it worm castings if you like that better," I say. "Even though it's really just plain old poop."

"Eww!" says Veronica Grace.

"Cool!" says Rupert.

"Can I help build the bench?" asks Alex.

"Sure thing," I say. "Bring your tool belt, because the worms are moving in tomorrow."

chapter 8

Grandma Barb brings her pickup truck to school right before morning recess the next day. She's already cut the pieces of wood we'll use to build the worm house. Annie, Rupert, Alex, and I help her carry them into the cafeteria.

Mrs. Grimes comes to help, too, but she doesn't really do anything. You can't get much done in clickety-clackety shoes, I guess. She says she'll supervise.

"Now, let's see." Grandma Barb puts her hands on her hips and looks around the cafeteria. "I don't think we'll want them by the window because it might get too hot in the sun." She points to the corner by the drinking fountain and garbage cans. "Right here will be perfect."

"Safety first!" says Alex. Alex is so excited about helping that he brought both of his toolboxes to school today. He reaches into the first one and pulls out four sets of safety goggles. He pulls one pair over his head. They're so big they cover his nose and most of his cheeks, too. He hands the other three pairs to Grandma Barb, Annie, and Rupert. Then he paws through his toolbox again, pulls out a pair of orange-and-green-striped swim goggles, and hands them to me. "Sorry," he says. "We were out of safety goggles. But Mick Buzzsaw says you should never start a project without protecting your eyes."

"This actually shouldn't take too long," Grandma Barb says, sliding two of the wood pieces together. "First, we need four nails right along here." She runs her hand along the edge of the wood, and Alex hammers.

Grandma Barb is right. It doesn't take long. We finish building just in time for the end of recess.

Mrs. Aloi brings the class in five minutes early so everyone can see the worms moving into their new house. Grandma Barb brings them in a big recycling bin from her truck. It's the same one Annie and I used to try and make paper. I can tell because Princess Margaret's head is still stuck to the inside.

"Gather 'round!" Grandma Barb says it in the same voice she uses when she has double chocolate chip cookies coming out of the oven or some other really terrific treat. "Here they are!"

Gently, she tips the bin and gives it a shake, and at first, it just looks like she's dumping tiny sticks and dirt and shredded newspapers into the worm house, but then I see the first little red squiggles riding the wave of dirt into their new home.

"Wow," Rupert says. "There's a bazillion of them."

"Actually, you're starting with about three thousand worms," Grandma says. "But they'll reproduce quickly. In a few weeks, if you look very closely, you'll start to see worm cocoons and then baby worms."

"Awesome!" says Rupert.

"Eww!" says Veronica Grace.

"Baby worms are cute," Annie tells her.

"No." Veronica Grace shakes her head. "Baby horses and baby lambs and baby giraffes like we saw at the zoo are cute. Baby worms are gross."

I'm glad there are no baby worms around yet to hear her and get their feelings hurt.

"Okay," says Grandma, tapping the recycling bin against the edge of the worm house so the very last worms spill out. "We're going to put the lid on now because worms like it dark. You can see how they've all wiggled down into the bedding material already."

I peek into the worm house and see a wormy tail disappear under a newspaper shred.

Grandma gives the bin one more tap, and Princess Margaret comes unstuck and lands on top of the worm bedding. I think about rescuing her, but I decide not to.

Princess Margaret looks like she'll be good at supervising.

chapter 9

We go back to our classroom for a math lesson before lunch, but nobody can really pay attention. Not with those worms wiggling around in the cafeteria, waiting to eat our leftover peas.

"Let's look at problem number one from your work sheet," Mrs. Aloi says.

"Do you think they eat carrots?" Rupert whispers to me. "I hate carrots."

"I think so. Grandma Barb says you can feed them any kind of food scraps except meat because it smells bad when it gets old and will stink up their house."

"My dad stinks up our house," Jimmy Lawson says. "When he goes in the bathroom with his *Sports Illustrated* after breakfast."

Mrs. Aloi shakes her maracas. "I can see you're excited about the worms, so let's do something different for math today. Let's say we have ten worms in our bin in the cafeteria, and each of those worms has two baby worms. How many worms will we have altogether?"

Jimmy Lawson raises his hand. "About ten million."

Mrs. Aloi raises her eyebrows. "Ten million? Are you doing the math, Jimmy?"

Jimmy looks all insulted. "I'm estimating."

"But it's not an estimating problem," Mrs. Aloi says. "Because you know there are ten worms to start. And then each one has two baby worms."

"Yeah, but those numbers are all wrong," Jimmy says. "We don't have ten worms. Marty's grandma says we have, like, three thousand right now. And they don't have two babies each. She told us they have whole big bunches of babies, and they're having babies, like, all the time, so

you wouldn't really be able to count the baby worms because by the time you were done counting, there'd be more baby worms, and by the time you counted those, the first bunch of baby worms would be having babies, too. So you'd need to estimate. And I estimate ten million." He smiles.

Mrs. Aloi looks at the clock and then looks at her little refrigerator in the corner where she puts her salad every day. I wonder if she's hungry or just excited to feed the worms her leftover lettuce.

"Those worms are the coolest," Jimmy says, and I smile.

I hope the Frog Lady thinks so, too.

🐛

Finally, it's lunchtime. The bringers go right to their tables with their lunch boxes. The buyers get in line, where Mrs. Baxter, the head cafeteria lady, serves hot dogs and Tater Tots and green beans, even if you don't want them.

Whenever they serve green beans, Jimmy Lawson asks if he can skip the beans, and Mrs. Baxter always says no. But today is different.

"May I please have extra green beans, Mrs. Baxter?" he says.

Mrs. Baxter draws her lips together like somebody fed her a lemon when she was expecting a strawberry. She squints her eyes at him. "You telling me you've become a fan of green beans all of a sudden, young man?"

He nods. "Kids need to eat five servings of fruits and vegetables each day," he tells Mrs. Baxter. "And so do worms," he whispers to me as we head for our table.

"Hey, everybody!" I call. "Don't forget that the worms are going to eat all our scraps, starting today, so we won't have to send any garbage to the landfill anymore *ever*," I say, even though I'm not positive it's true. It sounds exciting. "So save your leftovers!" I sit down at our table with Annie and Rupert and Alex to eat my hot dog and Tater Tots.

"Hey, Marty!" Rupert nudges me. "Isn't that your grandma?"

I look up, and sure enough, Grandma Barb is standing in the doorway, talking to Mrs. Grimes. I jump up and run over to her.

"Hi, Grandma! Did you come back to help us feed the worms?"

"Kind of." She gives me a quick hug. "I wanted to make sure your class understands how to care for them."

"Oh, we're all set," I tell her. "Jimmy even ordered extra green beans, so the worms will have plenty of food."

Grandma Barb looks at Mrs. Grimes. "That's what I was worried about," she says. "The worms can't have *too* much food while they're just getting used to their new home. We need to start slowly, and then as the worms reproduce and we have a bigger population, you'll be able to feed them more of your scraps."

"Oh," I say. I look over at the worm bin, where kids are already lined up. The buyers are standing there with big mounds of green beans on their trays. The bringers are all holding their sandwich crusts. "We may have a little extra food today, then."

Grandma walks to the front of the line. "Okay," she says. "The worms are still getting settled, so we can't give them too much work. Only a few of you will actually be able to add your lunch scraps today."

Isabel Pike steps up first with the crust of her tuna fish sandwich. Grandma sniffs it. "I don't think we want to put this in because it has tuna fish and mayonnaise all over it," she says. "Those things smell when they sit around too long. Does anyone have a peanut butter and jelly crust? That would work."

Isabel throws her crust in the garbage can and glares at me, like it's my fault her tuna fish smells.

Alex Farley steps up with his PB and J crust. "Should I break it up in little pieces for them?" he asks.

"You don't have to do that," Grandma says. She digs a little hole in the bedding material.

"Just put the crust in, and we'll cover it up." He drops the crust, and Grandma Barb brushes some newspaper shreds over it.

"That's it?" Alex says.

Grandma nods.

"Can't I watch them eat it?"

"Well, no," she says. "It will take them a long time. And they like it dark, so we'll put the lid back on when we're done."

"Hmph." Alex puts the rest of his garbage in the trash can and goes back to his table.

"Does anyone have extra vegetables?" Grandma Barb asks.

Every single one of the buyers raises their hands.

"Hmm. That's an awful lot of beans." Grandma points to Jimmy, who has a crazy huge mound of them on his tray. "Why don't you put about half of those in the bin for the worms?" she says.

Jimmy's mouth drops open. "But I got extras just for them!"

"That's not exactly the idea," Grandma says. She digs a little hole, and Jimmy puts in half his beans. Then she puts the lid back on the worm house. "That's all our worms can handle right now. In a few days, maybe we can start feeding them some more of your scraps."

I look down the line of trays with piles and

piles of green beans. My eyes move up the arms holding the trays until I get to the faces.

They are not happy, earth-saving faces. They are frowning faces.

And every last one is frowning right at me.

chapter 10

After lunch, we have project work time.

Veronica Grace and Isabel brought in little flower pots and seeds and a bag of dirt so they can grow their petunias. They're working over in the corner.

No, actually Isabel is working.

"Okay," Veronica Grace says. "Now pour some dirt into the pots."

Isabel pours.

"Now use your finger and poke a hole in the dirt in each pot."

Isabel pokes.

"And then drop two seeds in each hole."

Isabel drops the seeds.

"Brush a little dirt over them. And then water them."

Isabel brushes, and Isabel waters.

"Great," Veronica Grace says. "Mrs. Aloi! Mrs. Aloi! Look what I did! Look at my petunias, all ready to grow!"

"Lovely," says Mrs. Aloi. "Put them by the window." And she leaves to talk to Alex Farley.

"Put them by the window," Veronica Grace says.

Isabel puts.

Veronica Grace supervises.

"Alex and Rupert, I understand that you want to recycle these . . . these *things*." Mrs. Aloi looks at the collection of stuff people brought in and piled next to Alex's desk.

Five empty grape-juice bottles.

Two cardboard pizza boxes.

A hula hoop.

A faded blue-and-white-striped sheet.

Three poker chips.

A rusty metal lawn chair.

An old green garden hose.

And one straw hat that's falling apart but still has a pink ribbon and a little yellow bird on top.

"I like your idea very much," Mrs. Aloi tells them, "but we simply don't have the space to keep all of this in our classroom."

"Knock knock!" A man's standing at the classroom door with a rubber tire. "My son, Jimmy, forgot to bring this to school this morning."

"I'll take that." Rupert waves him over to his pile, and Mr. Lawson puts his tire next to the

hula hoop. "Thanks!" He turns to Mrs. Aloi. "That's the last of it. Really. And we promise we'll have our project together soon so it's out of the way."

"I'll tell everybody not to bring in any more." Alex calls to the class, "No more garbage, okay? We have what we need."

"Okay." Mrs. Aloi nods.

Alex turns to Rasheena and whispers, "Except for that old basketball you said you have. We still need that."

❧

"So I guess we should start writing in our observation journals," Annie says, holding the little notepad that Mrs. Aloi gave us after lunch. She said we could make observations whenever we want, but at least a couple times a week to start.

"Okay." I turn to the first page of my notepad and write:

Marty's Worm Journal - Day One

1. Built a worm house in the ~~cafateeria~~ ~~caffatiria~~ ~~cafatyrya~~ lunchroom.
2. Grandma dumped in worms. She says there are at least 3,000 worms.
3. Kids lined up to feed worms leftover green beans.
4. Not okay to feed worms tuna fish crust (smelly).
5. Not okay to feed worms more than a few dumb beans on the first day.
6. Everyone is mad at me.
7. That is so unfair.

I wish the worms were in here instead of the cafeteria so we could check on them more often. And I wish they did more than just wiggle around in the dark, eating garbage way too slow.

I watch Isabel poking holes in the dirt, and

Rasheena hooking up batteries and wires with Mrs. Aloi. I want to do something, too.

I raise my hand. "Mrs. Aloi? May I go to the cafeteria for just a minute?" If I say I just want to hang out with the worms, she'll for sure say no. "I'd like to make a few more observations for my journal."

"Sure." Mrs. Aloi smiles. "Just come right back."

I pick up my journal. "You coming?" I ask Annie, but Annie's journal entry is all done.

"No, thanks," she says. "I told Veronica Grace I'd help her water her flowers if I had time."

Well, fine. I'll go see the worms by myself.

The cafeteria is empty except for Mr. Klein, our school custodian, who's mopping the floor. He's tall and skinny and has a bald head except for two puffs of hair that stick out next to his ears.

"Good afternoon, Marty." He tips an imaginary hat at me and leans on his mop. "What brings you down here? Isn't lunch over?"

I nod. "I'm visiting the worms."

"I see. Is your project off to a good start?"

I think about the mountains of green beans that had to be thrown in the plain old regular garbage after lunch. "No," I tell him. "It's off to a terrible start. You can't give the worms too much food the first day, so not everybody got to feed them, and now they're all mad at me."

Mr. Klein walks over to the worm house and squats down next to me. "Seems to me your classmates need to understand these things take time." Mr. Klein lifts the lid off the worm house. We both watch as a whole bunch of little red bodies wiggle down into the newspaper bits and dirt.

I poke my finger down and find Alex's crust. It has some dirt stuck in the jelly, but otherwise, it looks exactly like it did at lunch. "It's taking so *long*."

Mr. Klein brushes some dirt and newspaper bits back over the crust and puts the lid back on the worm house. "You can't rush good work. Be patient, Marty."

I am not patient. My mom says "patient" and I are not even distant relatives. But I nod. "I'll try."

Mr. Klein goes back to mopping, and I pick up my journal. Before I head back to the classroom, I lift the lid on the worm house one more time.

"I'm being patient," I whisper inside. "But if you all could get moving on that crust tonight, it sure would be nice."

chapter 11

I try being patient.

Seriously. I do.

The whole next week, I go to lunch every day, and I do not even look in the direction of those worms. Not even once. I write three observation journal entries without even peeking, which is pretty clever if you ask me.

But there's just one problem. The journal entries I turn in to Mrs. Aloi at the end of the week are not very long.

Marty's Worm Journal – Day Five
1. Worm house is still in the corner of the ~~coffeeteria calfateerya~~ lunchroom.
2. Worms are probably working in the dark in there.

3. I wouldn't know.
4. Because I am busy being patient.

Marty's Worm Journal – Day Seven
1. Worm house is still there.
2. I am still ignoring it. Patiently.

Marty's Worm Journal – Day Nine
1. Worm house is still in the corner of the ~~lunchroom~~ cafeteria.
2. I looked up cafeteria in the dictionary this afternoon.
3. Because when you are being patient and not peeking at the worms, you have lots of extra time for things like that.

P.S. Do you think by Monday, a patient person would be able to open the lid to see what's going on in there?

Before going home Friday, I pull my worm journal out of my cubby and flip to my last entry to
see if Mrs. Aloi wrote back. She did:

> Checking the worms after the weekend sounds
> like a very good plan, Marty. You and Annie
> may visit them Monday morning.
> — Mrs. A

Waiting all weekend is as hard as waiting
for Christmas. I feel all squirmy and wondering. I can't wait to get back to school on
Monday.

I try to stay busy because Mom says that helps you be patient.

I fill the angry owl's water dish, even though I am not going near that thing to feed it.

I spend Sunday afternoon looking for crayfish with Annie. We catch three little ones in a bucket and then set them free. We patrol a little, too, but the woods are quiet again.

Finally, Monday morning comes, and I hurry to my classroom because my patience is all run out, and I can't wait to see what those worms have been up to. I bet they've finished all the food we gave them and will be ready to eat everybody's leftovers now.

I rush into class and say, "I'm going to check on the worms, okay?"

But no one answers. No one even says hi. The whole class is gathered around Veronica Grace's desk, oohing and ahhing.

"What's up?" I ask Annie.

"Veronica Grace and Isabel's petunias are up! That's what." Annie points into one of the little pots of dirt on the desk, and I can just see a skinny, scrawny little stem poking out with the seed still attached. It's all pale and wimpy looking.

"Well, that's not such a big deal," I say. "Come on. Let's go check on the worms."

"Not yet." Annie shakes her head. "I told Veronica Grace I'd do petunias, too, since we have to do a lot of waiting with the worms. Mrs. Aloi said I could be on both teams. I'm going to help water."

"Well, fine, but this team is going to check the worms now." I grab my worm journal and stomp out of the room and down the hall. I'm wearing my Jane Goodall hiking boots, which clunk extra loud, so all the second graders look up from their reading groups when I stomp by. I feel a little better by the time I get to the cafeteria.

"Morning!" says Mr. Klein. He's cleaning the windows with a long squeegee thing. "How are your worms?"

"I'm just checking on them now," I say, and lift the lid off their house.

At first, I'm a little worried because I can't see a single worm, but when I start poking around, they turn up. I poke my finger where Alex buried his sandwich crust but can't really find anything, and that makes my patient self very excited.

"Did you guys really eat it?" I poke some more. Still no PB and J crust. "Wow!"

I poke around the other side of the bin, where Jimmy dumped his green beans. Way at the bottom of the worm bin, I turn up a couple green bean stubs. One has a little red worm poking right through the middle of it.

"Hey, Mr. Klein! Mr. Klein! Look at this!" I wave him over and hold up the worm wearing the green bean. It looks like he's wiggled himself into a big fat hula hoop.

"Well, isn't that something?" Mr. Klein says. "They're good little workers, aren't they? See? They just needed a little time."

I put the lid back on the worm house, grab my journal, and skip down the hall to my classroom. Now that those worms are all settled and working, I'm going to have the coolest project.

Today, everybody can put in their peas and their crusts.

I cannot wait for lunch. Those worms are going to have the best feast ever.

chapter 12

When I get back to the classroom, Veronica Grace is lugging a watering can from the sink to her desk. Annie is up on a chair, holding one end of an old garden hose. Jimmy Lawson is on a chair a few feet away holding the other end. Alex and Rupert are duct-taping the middle of the hose to the top of a rusty aluminum lawn chair. Rasheena has some kind of buzzer going off in the corner. And Kimmy Butler is over in the reading area, hula-hooping.

"Don't break that!" Alex

yells at her from under the garden hose. "We need it for our top-secret, classified recycling project."

Mrs. Aloi is standing in the doorway, watching. She doesn't even try to quiet everybody down.

"Have you lost your maracas?" I ask her.

She shakes her head. "No, just my mind."

Kimmy hula-hoops into the side counter and knocks over the jar of crickets we feed our classroom lizard, Horace.

"That's it!" Mrs. Aloi yells, like she suddenly woke up and decided project time was over. "Put everything away and take out your math work sheets."

I'm worried the crickets are going to get squashed while everybody's cleaning up, so I rush over to scoop up as many as I can before they get out into the hallway. I must have missed a few, because I hear Miss Gail scream in the art room next door.

"Back to your seats now," Mrs. Aloi says, tugging on her skirt to straighten it. "You have the rest of our time before lunch to do problems one through ten."

I look down at my math work sheet. It's about a girl who has forty cents and wants to buy some candy necklaces that cost ten cents each.

We're supposed to figure out how many she can buy, but how am I supposed to concentrate on that when I have worm news that nobody's heard yet?

I'm about to raise my hand to ask about that, but Jimmy Lawson raises his first.

"Mrs. Aloi?"

"Yes?" Mrs. Aloi looks like she might need a nap.

"This math problem doesn't work."

"And why is that, Jimmy?"

"Because candy necklaces don't really cost ten cents each. They're at least fifty cents, and that's just for the crummy little ones that barely fit over your neck."

"Yeah," says Kimmy. "The good ones are a dollar, at least."

Mrs. Aloi shakes her maracas. I guess she found them while we were cleaning up. "Let's see who can do the problem just the way it is," Mrs.

Aloi says, "and we'll have a reward for the quietest worker." She points to the treat jar on her desk. It's full of tiny chocolate bars that she gives us when someone has done something really wonderful or when she just wants us to be good.

We work so quietly that everyone gets to take a treat for after lunch. I feel bad for the worms because with chocolate, there are never leftovers. The poor guys are always going to end up with just peas, beans, and crusts.

I hurry through the lunch line and thank Mrs. Baxter for the greenish-yellowish corn she piles next to my Monday veggie goulash. I quick eat my lunch, wrap my mushy corn and leftover goulash in a napkin, and head for the worm house.

"Hold on there." Mrs. Grimes clickety-clacks over to me from the cafeteria doorway. "I thought we were giving the worms a rest."

I nod. "We did. But they're done resting. They ate all the food, and they're ready for more."

Mrs. Grimes squints at me. "And you know how much they should have?"

I nod and lift the worm house lid. I dig in my finger and pull up a few wiggly little guys. "See? Don't they look hungry?"

Mrs. Grimes backs away. "I'll let you handle the feeding, then, Marty."

Before I can even get my corn and veggie goulash buried, there's a line of at least fifteen kids with trays at the worm house.

I stand up and smile. "The worms ate all their food from last week, so we're back in business. Who has crust?"

Every single person in line raises their hand.

"Okay," I say. "Let's get started."

Jimmy Lawson dumps all his corn into the bin.

Alex steps up with a PB and J crust that's perfectly square, like a picture frame. "Have a good lunch!" he tells the worms.

Kimmy's next. She has a whole tray full of veggie goulash and corn. "I just ate the ice cream," she says, and dumps everything else into the worm bin.

By the time we get to the last person in line, I'm having trouble finding places in the worm house that aren't already full of crust and corn and goulash, and I have to sort of shove the worms aside to make more room for food.

"Okay," I tell Isabel. "Go ahead and put in your crust."

Then I catch a sniff of fishiness.

"Hey, wait! Is that tuna fish? Grandma said no tuna fish because it smells."

Isabel puts her hands on her hips. "What good are your worms if they're such fussy eaters?"

"Oh, fine." I shove the crust into the hole I made and brush some corn on top of it.

"Time for third graders to go out for recess!" announces Mrs. Grimes.

I push down the lid of the worm house, but it almost doesn't fit because we added so much stuff today. I have to squish everything down more and pack it in to get the lid back on.

I sure hope those little guys are hungry.

chapter 13

As soon as I get to the classroom Tuesday morning, I know it is going to be a super bad day. It's bad enough that Veronica Grace is classroom helper this week. Now there are two rotten, terrible things on Mrs. Aloi's "Third-Grade Stars Today" list.

1. Today is Tuesday. State Reading Test!

2. No project time today due to testing!

What on earth are those exclamation points doing up there?

🐛

"Mrs. Aloi," I say after Veronica Grace finishes leading the Pledge of Allegiance. "I know there's

no real project time today, but we gave the worms a lot of food yesterday, and I'm wondering how they're doing, so do you think I could just —"

"Did you read what it says on the board, Marty?"

"Well, yes."

"Good." She shakes her maracas. "Let's go! We have to get you through the first section of the reading test before lunch."

She hands me my test, and I go back to my seat.

I put my name on my test and answer sheet.

I read the passages and answer the questions.

I fill in the bubbles so there is no white space left because if you leave any white space, you get it wrong even if you got it right.

Finally, Veronica Grace collects our test papers so we can go to lunch.

She's classroom helper, so she gets to be line leader, too, which drives me crazy because I just want to get there and see how the worms are doing.

"I like the way Veronica Grace is leading us to lunch, with quiet, walking feet," Mrs. Aloi says.

But when we get to the cafeteria, Veronica Grace's quiet, walking feet turn into screaming, running-back-down-the-hall feet.

"EEEEEEWWWWW!"

I rush into the lunchroom to see what Mrs. Baxter could possibly be serving to make Veronica Grace run like that. But then I realize it isn't lunch that made her scream.

The worms have escaped.

"Dude, watch out!" Jimmy Lawson pushes Alex Farley away from the bin. "You just stepped on one."

"Ewww!" Isabel and Kimmy take off down the hall after Veronica Grace.

Annie squats down next to the bin and starts scooping up worms. "Come on, Marty. We've got

to get them off the floor, or they're all going to get squashed."

I scoop up the worms that are hanging out together in clumps, but most of them are stretched out long and skinny and sliding along the smooth cafeteria floor tiles, and that makes them hard to pick up. They're slippery, too.

"Everyone go sit down," Mrs. Aloi says. "Go . . . have your lunch, and let Marty and Annie take care of the worms." She looks at me. "I'm going to the office to call your grandmother. She *told* us the worms would be no problem."

Annie and I have missed half our lunch period by the time we get the last worm back into its worm house and wash our hands.

"Come on, girls," Mrs. Baxter says. "I know you're late, but you gotta eat something." She hurries us back to the serving line and loads up our trays with food.

"Thanks," I say, and go to my seat, but I don't feel like eating. My stomach is all tied up in knots. Plus, even though I washed my hands, they still feel all wormy.

When I look down, what I see on my tray doesn't help my appetite one bit.

Spaghetti.

chapter 14

Annie finishes and runs off to help Veronica Grace water petunias. The petunias have not escaped. The petunias are doing exactly what they are supposed to do.

I sit and stare at my spaghetti worms.

Grandma Barb's truck pulls into the driveway in front of the school while I'm finishing my milk. She comes in, talks to Mrs. Grimes and Mrs. Aloi in the doorway, and then walks right over to me.

"I hear you had some excitement today."

I nod. "Bad excitement."

"I thought the worms were doing fine," she says.

"They were."

"Did you check on them yesterday?"

"Yep. They'd eaten everything we gave them last week."

"Did you give them more food?"

"Yep."

"How much more?"

I look down at my tray full of spaghetti. "I meant to give them just a little every day like you said, but everybody was lined up, and they were so happy they finally got to feed the worms that I guess I . . . I forgot."

Grandma walks over to the worm house and lifts the lid. She pokes around inside and pulls out some crusts, along with a big handful of Kimmy's veggie goulash and mushy corn. She picks out a few worms, drops them back in their house, and puts the food into the garbage can. She takes out more goulash noodles. More corn. Some bread crust, which she sniffs and then frowns at. Must be Isabel's tuna fish. Finally, she walks back over and sits down next to me.

"Marty, the worms burrowed down and found a way to escape because their environment became inhospitable."

"What's inhospitable?"

"A lousy place to be."

"Oh."

"Remember how we talked about feeding them a little every day?" Grandma says.

"Now I do." I doubt the worms will ever want to eat food from me again.

"You can't overdo it from now on, okay?"

"Okay." I look at the line of kids with leftover spaghetti forming by the worm house. "Does that mean no scraps for them today?"

Grandma nods.

"Will you tell them?" I ask her.

She shakes her head. "Nope. Explaining the rules — and the reasons for the rules — is part of your project." She kisses me on my head and leaves.

I look over and see Jimmy lifting the lid off the worm house, ready to scoop in his whole serving of spaghetti.

"Hold on!" I leave my tray on the table and run over to the worm corner. "It turns out we can't feed them today."

"Why not?" Jimmy frowns at his mound of spaghetti. "I saved this for them special."

"Yeah," Isabel says. "You told us they could eat, like, everything from now on."

"You said we wouldn't have lunch scraps in the garbage anymore," Kimmy says. She tips her tray and some peas roll off onto the floor. "You said no more garbage in the landfill. Not ever."

I take a deep breath. "I . . . got excited and . . . maybe kind of . . . imagined they were superworms. But they're not."

Alex looks at the crust in his hand. "Are they ever going to be able to eat all of our lunch garbage like you said?"

"I don't think so." I sound like a worm when the tiny little words come out of my mouth. "At least not for a really long time."

"Hmph." Isabel clunks her tray against the edge of the garbage can, and her spaghetti slides off with a big plop. Jimmy's spaghetti mountain goes next, in a big, mushy landslide. *Plop!*

One by one, they dump their trays and walk past, frowning at me. And who can blame them?

I am a big fat worm liar who is never going to save the earth.

Not ever.

chapter 15

"Aren't you supposed to be outside at recess?" Mr. Klein finds me in my top-secret hiding spot, which is also his mop closet, it turns out.

"I came in here because my environment became inhospitable," I tell him.

"I see." He leans his mop in the corner. "Is this, by any chance, about the worm slime I just mopped off the cafeteria floor?"

I nod. "They got out because I let everybody feed them so much, and it made their worm house a lousy place to live."

Mr. Klein reaches for his lunch box on the top shelf.

"So are they back inside their worm castle, safe and sound now?"

I sigh. "We put them back, and my grandma

took out the extra food, but now we can't feed them anymore, and everybody hates me."

Mr. Klein scratches the puff of hair over his ear. Then he opens his lunch box and pulls out a small bag of raisins. "Want some?" He holds it down to me.

"Sure." I take three because they're small. They taste different from the ones Mom buys in

boxes at the grocery store. Fruitier. "These are really good."

"They come from grapes I grow myself," he says, and pops a raisin in his mouth. "It took the vine three years to start growing fruit." He hands me the bag again. I take two more raisins.

"Three *years*? That means I was in kindergarten when you planted it."

Mr. Klein smiles. "They're worth every day I waited, don't you think?"

I nod. They're the best raisins ever.

"Time for you to go outside and get some fresh air." He reaches down to help me up. "Patience, Marty. You let those worms of yours do things on their own time, and you'll end up saving the earth just fine."

chapter 16

Marty's Worm Journal – Day Twenty-three

1. This will be an extra-long journal entry to make up for the one I didn't do last week, when things were not going so well.

2. Things are going better now. Worms have not escaped since last Tuesday.

3. The reason they escaped was because their environment was inhospitable back then.

4. Because I let everybody feed them too much.

5. Even tuna fish that smelled.

6. A plan to prevent future disasters is in place.

I think Mr. Klein is the smartest person at Orchard Street Elementary School. I don't know why they don't make him principal. Plus, he wears sneakers instead of clickety-clackety shoes, so he could get places a lot faster than Mrs. Grimes.

After last week's Great Worm Escape, Mr. Klein helped Annie and me set up two buckets next to the garbage cans in the cafeteria. One is really small, like the kind of beach bucket you use for the very top of a sand castle tower where it gets skinny. That one is food for the worms every day, and Annie and I will sort through it just to make sure there's no bad-smelling tuna or anything. When that first bucket is full, kids get to dump their food scraps in the other bucket, which is a lot bigger.

At the end of every day, Mr. Klein takes the bigger bucket out back and empties it into the brand-new compost pile he started for us next to the Dumpster. He says out there, our garbage will turn into good stuff for the earth, too. So we really do get to send less to the landfill.

And the worms don't have to worry about eating it all themselves. Because that was a lot of pressure to put on those little guys.

"You know," Annie says, digging a hole for Kimmy's leftover salad, "these worms could probably use some new newspaper shreds and stuff."

I poke through the bedding and see she's right. Some of it is gone, replaced by really dark, black dirt. "You're right! Let's ask Mrs. Aloi if we can clean out their house tomorrow and give them more newspaper."

"And we can use the castings as fertilizer." Annie drops the lettuce into the bin.

"What are we going to fertilize?" I brush dirt and stuff over the crust to cover it up.

"Well . . . I was thinking maybe we could use it to fertilize Veronica Grace's petunias!"

"Yeah, *right*," I say. "There's no way she'll let you put worm poop in her precious petunia plants."

"No, I guess not."

I scoop up a handful of dirt. Well, worm castings, actually, but it's hard to think of it that way since it looks just like really nice garden soil. It looks like the stuff Mom buys at Gregory's Green Garden Center.

As a matter of fact, if you put this stuff in a fancy bag . . .

"Annie," I say.

"Yeah?"

"I think maybe Veronica Grace will be interested in our fertilizer after all."

chapter 17

Annie and I work all weekend to get the labels just right on the computer.

"You're certainly putting a lot of time into this school project, girls," Mom says. "Finish up soon. Grandma Barb is bringing over dinner and eating with us."

"We're almost done," I say, "but it needs to be really good, or it won't work." I move the picture on the screen over a little so it sits right underneath the words we typed in. "All set. 'Black Gold. Magic for your plants.' It's perfect!"

Annie leans in to look. "Print it," she says.

I press the button and tap my fingers on the desk while the printer spits out the paper with our perfect fancy-fertilizer labels.

"We need some small print, too, telling what's in it," I say.

"Well, we can't exactly do that, can we?" Annie says. "I don't think you're allowed to lie on labels."

"No, I'm pretty sure they haul you off to jail for that."

"Dinner is served!" Grandma Barb's voice booms down the hall. "A gourmet blend of specially aged cheeses, the finest whole grains, vine-ripe tomatoes, and just a touch of expertly cured meat, seasoned to perfection."

I run to the kitchen and find her carrying a pepperoni pizza from Tony's in one hand and a big bottle of Lemon-Lime-Fizzy-Whiz soda in the other.

"Pizza? You said all that stuff, and it's just pizza?"

She holds up the Fizzy-Whiz. "And a sparkling citrus beverage for extra refreshment."

Annie catches up to me and Grandma, and all three of us laugh. "You can make anything sound wonderful if you describe it the right way," Grandma Barb says.

I look at Annie. Annie looks at me. "Anything?" I say.

🐛

It doesn't take long for Grandma Barb to help us think up the right words for a great-sounding-and-still-not-exactly-a-lie worm-poop label.

I print out another sheet, stick a label on a paper lunch bag, and read it aloud. "Black Gold. Magic for your plants. This fabulously balanced blend of organic carbon, nitrogen, phosphates, and potassium will jump-start your junipers and put pep in your petunias. Your plants will love Black Gold, and you will, too!"

"Perfect!" Grandma Barb says.

We head back to the kitchen for our specially aged cheeses, finest whole grains, vine-ripe tomatoes, and expertly cured meat. It's still hot — and it tastes as delicious as it sounds.

BLACK GOLD

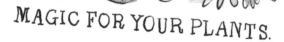

MAGIC FOR YOUR PLANTS.

This fabulously balanced blend of organic carbon, nitrogen, phosphates, and potassium will jump-start your junipers and put pep in your petunias. Your plants will love BLACK GOLD, ❀ and you will, too! ❀

chapter 18

Marty's Worm Journal - Day Thirty

1. Only a few more days until Amelia Ranidae comes back and we find out who wins the contest!!

2. (That was not really an observation. Sorry. I just got excited.)

3. Worms are still staying in their house.

4. Burrowing observation - when I lift the lid, they burrow down to the bottom. Grandma Barb says this is because they don't like the light.

5. Most of this week's food scraps are gone, except for the peach pit that I told Jimmy not to put in there in the first place.

6. We took some of the worm castings out of the bin ~~and put them in fancy fer-~~ ~~tilizer bags so we could trick Veronica~~ ~~into thinki~~ and added more shredded newspaper.

Phew! That was almost a huge mistake. Annie and I promised to keep our Black Gold a total secret because the trick is already working so well.

On Monday, we brought the paper bag to school, filled it with worm castings, and then borrowed tape from the secretary in the office to seal it all up.

Veronica Grace came skipping down the hall, wearing a new purple dress with big pink flowers that look like her petunias are supposed to look someday. She went right for the bag in Annie's hand.

"What's that?"

"Black Gold," Annie said, and read Veronica Grace the label.

"Oh, Annie!" she said. "Can we use some of this on the petunias? Please? Then they'll be big and bright and beautiful, and we'll win for sure. Oh, please?" Annie nodded. "You are the greatest science project partner in the world!" Veronica Grace grabbed the bag and ran off down the hall.

I add another observation to my list, even though Mrs. Aloi won't understand what it has to do with the worms right now.

7. Veronica Grace's petunias are growing quite nicely. She must have great fertilizer.

I'm about to put down my pencil when I remember one more thing I wanted to write.

8. Little brown balloon thingys in the dirt. What are they?

When the clock ticks to lunchtime, I bring my journal with me to the cafeteria, just in case there are any new observations.

Grandma Barb is talking with Mrs. Grimes when I get there, so I rush right over and give her a fast, hard hug that surprises her so much she almost tips over.

"Well, hi there, Worm Girl!" she says. "I hear things have been going very, very well. I told Mrs. Grimes I'd keep an eye on the bin so we wouldn't have any more breakouts."

I look at my sneakers and wish everybody would quit talking about that. Then I remember about the balloon thingys.

"Hey, Grandma — I need to show you something in the worm bin, okay?"

"It's not a week-old tuna sandwich, is it?" She follows me to the bin, and I lift the lid.

"Hold on." I paw through the bedding stuff and move aside a banana peel. "They're in here somewhere." I spot one of the little balloon things and push it onto my fingertip. "See that?" I hold it up. "What is it?"

"Well, bust my buttons!" she says. "You're going to be a grandmother, Marty!"

"A grandmother?"

Grandma pokes around in the bin some more. "Oh, look, they're all over the place. Oh, this is just fantastic." She brushes off her hands. "Your worms are having babies, Marty. This . . ." She points to the tiny ball on my finger. ". . . is a cocoon."

"A cocoon? Does that mean the worm is going to change into a butterfly?"

Grandma smiles and shakes her head. "No, it's more like an egg, actually. Baby worms will hatch from there when the time is right."

"Babies? The worms are having babies?"

"Yep. Congratulations, Grandma Marty."

Gently, so I don't damage it, I slide the cocoon back into the bin. I'm going to have grandsons and granddaughters.

Or a bunch of grandworms, at least.

chapter 19

The day before our contest ends is crazy busy because everybody's trying to finish, and everybody's wondering which project is going to win.

I'm a little worried. The Frog Lady is coming back tomorrow, and all I have to show her is a bunch of half-eaten carrot sticks and worm poop.

Alex's recycled lady looks really cool, and Veronica Grace's petunias are growing like crazy now, and whatever Rasheena is doing with the buzzers and batteries seems to be working, too.

I don't know who's going to win the contest, but I do know this: No one ever saved the world with half-eaten carrot sticks and worm poop.

Plus, I still don't know what I'm going to wear to school for the big day. Mrs. Aloi says everybody can wear a costume with an environmental theme to the assembly.

"What are you going to be?" I ask Annie after lunch while we're sorting out which food scraps to give to the worms.

"A cat," she says.

"A cat?"

"Yep."

"That doesn't have anything to do with the environment."

Annie tosses an apple core into the corner of the worm bin. "I know, but when I told my mom our costumes had to be about the environment, she said she already made me two costumes this year — the cat for Halloween and that bluebird suit I wore for the play, and I should be one of those."

"So you're just going to ignore the theme?"

Annie shrugs, sniffs a sandwich crust, and throws it in the garbage. It must have been tuna. "I'll figure something out. What about you?"

"I'm not sure. But Grandma Barb is coming over tonight. I bet she'll help."

Annie pokes some of the worm bedding aside to make room for a new banana peel. "I know!" she says. "I have a perfect idea!"

"Yeah?"

"You should dress up as a composting worm!"

chapter 20

Five hours later, I am starving and dying of thirst.

But I cannot eat or drink because I am wrapped in wet cardboard, panty hose, and duct tape.

"Just hold still there, Worm Girl!" Grandma Barb reaches behind my back with a giant stapler to connect the two edges of soggy cardboard wrapped around me. I hope she doesn't staple it to my bottom. "There!" she says. "See if you can still move your arms."

I wiggle my arms, but they're mostly pinned to my side because I am wrapped in so many layers of worminess.

When I told Grandma Barb what Annie suggested, she did the jazzy little project dance she does whenever anyone asks for her help. Then she took me out to the garage, and we cut up a box and soaked it in the tub so we could bend the cardboard. Grandma wrapped it around me and pulled panty hose over my head, and now she's making the whole outfit tighter and squeezier so when I go to school tomorrow dressed like a worm, I will stay that way all day long.

"Hold still again." She grabs her scissors, cuts off a long piece of duct tape, and smooths it around my waist. "There. Now we can see your sections."

"Grandma?" I say through the panty hose. "I can't really breathe."

"Hmm. Hold still." She uses the scissors to cut me a nose hole, which helps. A little.

Then she cuts a hole in each side of my cardboard worm body.

"What are these holes for?"

"For your arms, silly."

"But worms don't have arms!"

"True." Grandma Barb pulls one of my hands out each hole. "But worms don't have math problems to do, either. You'll need your hands free."

That is about the most ridiculous thing I've heard, but I don't tell Grandma Barb because I don't want to hurt her feelings. Instead, I use my worm arms — just this once — to grab the duct tape and sneak it into my backpack.

chapter 21

"Today is the big day — the end of our Save the Earth contest," Mrs. Aloi reminds us when she meets us outside to walk us down to the third-grade hallway. "And look at all of these terrific earth-saving costumes!"

"Hurry up!" I tell Rupert. He's dressed as the sun to represent solar energy. "Just wrap the duct tape around me so you can't see my arms."

Rasheena is wearing a blue recycling bin held up by suspenders. It's filled with empty milk jugs and cans. "This is our old one. My mom cut holes for my legs and helped me fill it up." She holds up a tomato soup can.

Veronica Grace is at the front of the line, wearing a floofy pink dress with big pink feathery things sticking out all around her neck.

She has on a yellow baseball hat, bright green tights that make her legs look extra skinny, and brown shoes.

"And what do we have here?" Mrs. Aloi bends down to see Veronica Grace's costume better.

"I'm a petunia," says Veronica Grace. She holds up one brown shoe. "These are my roots!" She points to one green knee. "And this is my stem."

"How come you got two stems?" Jimmy asks. "That's kinda weird."

Veronica Grace purses her lips and stands very straight, with her legs pressed close together. "There. If I stand like this, I only have one stem. Now can you tell I'm a petunia?"

"You're a lovely petunia," Mrs. Aloi says, and steps up to Annie, who's next in line. "And you are . . . a cat?"

Annie nods and holds up a small cardboard

sign strung around her neck that says DR. JANE GOODALL'S CAT.

"Very creative," says Mrs. Aloi, and Annie gives me the thumbs-up sign.

Alex Farley is next, and he's wearing a cardboard box with five long, flat pieces of wood sticking out from a circle in the middle. "Spin me!" he tells Mrs. Aloi. "Go ahead. I built it so it really works."

She reaches out to one of the long, wood pieces and pulls down on it. Alex's whole front spins around and around. "I'm a wind generator!" he says. "I can generate enough electricity for five hundred families."

"Really?" asks Annie.

"Well, not me, personally," Alex says, "because we couldn't quite get the connections to work. But the big wind turbines you see up on hills can do that."

"Wow," Mrs. Aloi says. "And what are you, Marty?"

"A worm," I say, but it comes out all muffled because the mouth-hole in my panty-hose mask is out of place. I'd adjust it, but my arms are duct-taped to my body.

"A worm?"

I nod and try to say "a composting worm," but it comes out more like "a hrmfsting hrm."

Mrs. Aloi looks at me. "Where are your arms?"

I look down and try to wiggle one. The duct tape wrinkles a tiny bit.

"Oh dear. Let's get you to the nurse's office to get untaped." She reaches for my hand, but worms don't have hands, so she ends up just kind of pushing me down the hallway to the nurse, who shakes her head and gets to work untaping.

When I get back to class, I have arms again, and everyone is doing their last journal entry before the contest ends. I look around at everyone writing like crazy. They all have lots to say about their projects and cool costumes. Not like me. But I have arms now and no excuse not to write, so I pull out my pencil.

Marty's Final, Last Worm Journal – Day Thirty-four

1. Worms are probably the same as yesterday.
2. But I can't say for sure.
3. Because I haven't seen them today.
4. I was in the nurse's office getting duct tape pulled off my arms.
5. I know Grandma Barb loves duct tape, but the stuff is a lot easier to put on than it is to take off.

P.S. I sure hope our worms win the contest!

chapter 22

All the rest of the morning, I stare at the only thing on Mrs. Aloi's "Third-Grade Stars Today" list. It has FOUR exclamation points.

1. After gym class: Amelia Ranidae assembly to announce Save the Earth winners!!!!

But it doesn't feel like it's worth even one exclamation point anymore. What chance do I possibly have of winning?

Alex and Rupert have their giant sculpture made of recycled materials under a big sheet in the corner. They borrowed a cart from Mr. Klein's custodian closet to get it down to the auditorium.

Rasheena has some fancy, buzzing, electronic recycling gizmo.

Veronica Grace has her petunias all lined up on her tray, ready to carry them down when it's time for our assembly. One of them is just about to bloom.

"Is your display all ready, Marty?" Veronica Grace asks as she sniffs her almost-petunia.

"Yep. Right here." I hold up my paper cup full of worm poop so she can wrinkle her nose. I might as well get used to it.

We stop at the auditorium on the way to gym and drop our projects off on the stage so Amelia Ranidae can look them over and make her final decisions about winners.

We're supposed to be doing a basketball unit in gym, but everybody's costumes get in the way. Annie trips over her tail, and I can't really get around very well, either. Basketball is hard for worms. Even worms with arms.

Finally, gym class ends, and Mrs. Aloi picks us up and walks us to the auditorium. Mrs. Grimes stands in front and reminds everyone to sit carefully, but she's too late because two kindergarten boys are already crocodile-snapped and stuck with their feet sticking up. Their teachers help them out, and finally, it's quiet enough for Mrs. Grimes to introduce our guest.

"It is my pleasure to welcome back Amelia Ranidae," she says, and the Frog Lady walks onstage. She must have left her poison dart frogs at home this time, because all she's holding is a box of trophies.

"Good morning," she says. "Today's the day you've been waiting for. I've had a chance to review your projects. You've done outstanding work, and it's been difficult for me to choose just a handful of winners. I'm going to ask those students to come forward and say a few words about their projects."

She takes forever to go through the winners for kindergarten, first, and second grade. I try to sit still in my chair, but I'm all excited and itchy under my worm costume.

"And now, the winning projects for third grade." Everyone gets quiet. The Frog Lady takes a deep breath. "Alex Farley and Rupert Wingfield . . . Rasheena Wells . . . and finally, Veronica Grace Smithers and her partners Isabel Pike and Annie Thomas."

Everyone claps. Even me. I make my hands do it even though the rest of me is mad. I guess I didn't really expect to be up there showing off my worm poop, but I can't believe Veronica Grace's stupid petunias won.

"Alex and Rupert, would you show us your project?" The Frog Lady moves the microphone down so he can reach.

"Absolutely," says Alex. He pulls a little slip of paper with notes out of his tool belt. "My fellow students, we throw away so many plastic and metal items that could have new lives if only we were more creative. Over the past few weeks, you've been bringing us some of the junk from your house, and we've made it into . . ." He signals to Rupert, who pulls the sheet off the sculpture with a flourish. "Super-Earth-Woman!"

Underneath the sheet is a . . . well . . . sort of a cross between a robot and a scarecrow wearing a dress. It has a rusty lawn-chair body that flares out into a giant hula-hoop skirt with a blue-and-white-striped pattern. Juice bottles stuck on straightened-out coat hangers stretch out of the lawn chair as arms. Super-Earth-Woman has flat cardboard pizza-box feet. And her head is a deflating basketball with a poker-chip nose and eyes and a straw hat with a pink ribbon and a little yellow bird on top.

"Wow," Amelia Ranidae says. "That's really something."

Alex grins. "I think she looks kind of like you."

Amelia Ranidae gives Alex and Rupert their trophies and then calls Rasheena up to the microphone. She shows pictures and explains the new recycling system she set up for her family in the kitchen. "And now," Rasheena says, "it's set up so if my dad throws any more aluminum cans away in the regular trash, there's a metal detector that will set off an alarm like this." She demonstrates her buzzer. "I really wanted to set it up so he'd

get zapped with a shock, too, like those electric dog fences, but my mom said I couldn't."

"Congratulations," Amelia Ranidae says, handing Rasheena a trophy. "Your project shows a real commitment to recycling."

Finally, Annie, Isabel, and Veronica Grace come forward. Veronica steps up to the microphone while Isabel holds the two biggest petunia plants in front of her.

"Good morning, everyone," Veronica Grace says, smiling. "I'm sure no one is surprised to see me here, given how beautifully our petunias have grown. So I'd like to say just a few words of thanks . . ."

Veronica Grace has been watching too many TV award shows, because she goes on for about five minutes, thanking her mother and her father and the mailman who brought the pots they ordered special from the garden supply store in Tennessee. The whole time she talks, Isabel is wrinkling her nose and holding the petunia plants farther and farther away from her.

"And finally, I offer my greatest thanks to —"

"Yeeeee-EWWWWWW!" Isabel drops the petunia to the stage floor and starts shaking her hand like something bit her. "Ewwwww!! Worm slime!!!" She runs offstage.

"Worm slime?" Amelia Ranidae tilts her head as Veronica Grace bends to pick up the plant.

"Ewwwww!!!" Veronica Grace jumps up from the spilled mud and follows Isabel, and suddenly, I know what happened. Annie and I were so careful when we packaged our Black Gold fertilizer; we tried to pick every single little worm out of the castings. But we forgot about the cocoons. The baby worms must have hatched themselves right into Veronica Grace's petunia plants.

Annie bends down to scoop the spilled dirt and the poor petunia plant back into the pot. She pauses, smiles at one of the clumps of dirt, then scoops it into the pot, too. She stands on her tiptoes to whisper something to the Frog Lady.

"Ohhh . . ." the Frog Lady says, and then listens some more. Finally, she nods and heads to the microphone. "Marty McGuire, would you join us onstage as well?"

At first, I think I'm about to get in trouble in

front of the whole school, but when I get to the steps, I see a big smile on the Frog Lady's face, so I join Annie and peek into the petunia pot.

Sure enough, I can see the tail ends of three tiny worms disappearing into the dirt. I'm a grandmother.

"If I might have your attention again . . ." the Frog Lady says, and the kids all get quiet. "I've just learned that there was more to this lovely petunia plant than meets the eye. It's been fertilized for the past two weeks with worm castings from your cafeteria worm farm." She lifts the tiny, pink petunia blossom with two fingers. "And I think you can all see how beautifully that's worked out, even if our petunia grower didn't quite know what was in her fertilizer." She lifts two trophies from her box and hands one to Annie. "These two young ladies have illustrated perhaps the most important lessons of all when it comes to saving the earth. One — that you need to be . . .

creative sometimes." She hands me the second shiny gold trophy. The top part is a sculpture of a hand holding a globe that really spins. "And two," the Frog Lady says, "working together is the only way we're going to get the job done."

Annie grins and high-fives me, and we both look down at the petunias and dirt and baby worms. I'd high-five them, too, but worms don't have arms.

Instead, I whisper, "Good job, little guys!" and head back to my seat.

chapter 23

I get a ride home with Annie's mom and can hardly wait to show Mom and Dad my trophy. I wish it had a worm on it, but a spinning earth is almost as good.

"I'll see you right after dinner?" Annie tosses her backpack over her shoulder and heads for her porch.

"You bet!" We have big plans to celebrate our earth-saving greatness with a dessert picnic out by the creek. It's not a big, fancy thing like Jane Goodall has when she wins awards for saving the environment, but it's going to be great. Annie's mom stopped at the store on the way home and got us brownie mix and gummy worms. If you ask me, a brownie-and-gummy-worm picnic with the crayfish is better than a fancy-schmancy awards ceremony anyway.

I wave at Annie and head for the porch just as Grandma Barb's car pulls into the driveway. I rush right over.

"Grandma Barb! Look! Annie and I won an earth-saving award!" I run right up to her and jump up and down with my trophy.

"Hold it still a minute!" Grandma Barb takes my trophy hand, and I stop jumping so she can see. "Well, how about that! Those worms came through for you after all."

Just then, Mom comes out to the porch, wearing her extra-thick gloves that reach up to her elbows. "Dinnertime for the Evil One." She holds up a jar of fat crickets and walks toward the owl's cage with a determined look on her face.

Grandma Barb opens the back door of the

car and pulls out a big flat pizza box. "It's a busy-mom dinner night," she says. Busy-mom dinner nights are my favorite.

"I hope the angry owl lives with us forever so we can have pizza every week," I say, but before the words make it out of my mouth, Mom calls us out back.

"I thought you might like to say good-bye." She's wearing her heaviest gloves, holding the owl by its feet. "She's all better and ready to go."

The owl still looks angry to me, but maybe it's just because she's not free yet.

"Ready?" Mom asks, and we help her count. "One . . . two . . . three . . ." There's a crazy big whoosh of enormous wings flapping, and we watch as the owl turns into a dark shadow flying off into the woods.

Mom sighs. "The funny thing is, I'm going to miss her." She sees the pizza box in Grandma's arms and sniffs at it. "Are there mushrooms on here?"

Grandma Barb nods. "Double mushrooms."

"And a fabulous blend of specially aged cheeses," I add.

And we all head inside for what might be the last busy-mom pizza night for a while.

🐛

"Don't be long," Mom says as I pack two apple-juice boxes in my lunch box with one of those keep-it-cold freezery things. "It's going to get dark soon."

I nod and skip down the path through the woods to the creek to meet Annie. She's already waiting by the big rock with two paper plates. On each one is a tangle of gummy worms, nesting on top of a brownie that's still warm. I hop up onto the rock and reach for a worm.

"Hold on!" Annie says. "We should give speeches. Jane Goodall always gives a speech when she gets a big award."

That sounds a lot like homework to me, but Annie seems excited, so I nod. "Okay. What sort of stuff does Jane Goodall usually say?"

"Hmmm . . ." Annie picks up a dry, brown leaf and twirls it between her fingers. "She thanks people. And she says how much she loves her chimpanzees. And that's about it." She looks at me. "You go first."

"Okay," I say. "Thanks, Annie, because you helped a whole lot with —"

"Not like that!" Annie gives me a little push. "You have to stand up and pretend you're in front of like a million people and talk fancy. Like 'I am grateful to accept this award, and I would like to thank . . .' and then start saying all the names."

"All the names?" I was planning to thank Annie and eat that red-and-orange gummy worm.

She nods. I stand up straight and grab a pine-cone to use as my microphone.

"Ladies and gentlemen, it is my great pleasure to accept this award for saving the earth. I'd like to thank my wormy, earth-saving teammate, Annie, and . . . um . . ." *Who else can I thank?* "Mrs. Aloi for assigning the project. And that's all."

"What about Veronica Grace?" Annie says.

"I'm not thanking her!"

Annie tips her head at me. "But she is the one who made everyone notice the worms today."

I smile a little, remembering the back of her head as she ran out of the auditorium. "Okay, thanks to Veronica Grace, too," I say very fast.

"Now can we eat?" I ask Annie.

"Wait, I have to give my speech, too," Annie says. She looks out over the trees as if

there's a whole crowd of squirrels listening. "I'd like to thank Mrs. Aloi and Veronica Grace and Isabel, and the Frog Lady, too. And my mom and dad. And especially my best friend, Marty."

She nods, and I pull out the juice boxes. We put our straws in and try to "cheers" with them the way they did with the fancy, clinky glasses at my aunt's wedding. Juice boxes don't clink, though. They just sort of thump quietly.

"Oh, well. Cheers!" Annie holds up her gummy worm, and I hold up one of mine. We "cheers" with our worms, and even though they don't clink, either, it's a perfect celebration.

"To the worms!" Annie says. And she bites off the green one's head.

"To the worms!" I say, and I pop the whole red-and-orange one into my mouth.

The sun's sprinkling its last little bits of brightness through the trees, so we finish our dessert picnic and head home.

"Want to take one more lap on earth-saving patrol?" Annie asks.

I nod, and we set off. We are earth-saver superheroes, checking behind every tree. But there's not a bad guy with an ax in sight.

They know better than to mess with Annie and me.

Kate Messner is the author of *The Brilliant Fall of Gianna Z.*, winner of the E. B. White Read Aloud Award for Older Readers; *Sugar and Ice*; *Sea Monster's First Day*; *Over and Under the Snow*; and *Marty McGuire*. A former middle-school English teacher, Kate lives on Lake Champlain with her family and loves reading, walking in the woods, and traveling. Visit her online at www.katemessner.com.

Brian Floca is the author and illustrator of *Moonshot: The Flight of Apollo 11* and *Lightship*, both Sibert Honor Books. Before creating the pictures for *Marty McGuire*, he illustrated Avi's award-winning Poppy series, and Jan Greenberg and Sandra Jordan's *Ballet for Martha: Making Appalachian Spring*, which earned him a third Sibert Honor. Brian grew up in Texas and now lives in Brooklyn, New York. Find him online at www.brianfloca.com.

TURN THE PAGE FOR A SNEAK PEEK
AT MARTY'S FIRST ADVENTURE:

marty
mcguire

That nice Mrs. Kramer lied to me about third grade.

On the last day of school, she gave us cupcakes with sprinkles and little beach umbrellas and said have a super-duper summer and she'd wave to us in the hallway next year. She said third grade would be even more fun than second grade. She said we'd read bigger books and keep our old friends and make new ones and even get to be in the school play.

None of it is true. Because Veronica Grace Smithers has stolen my best friend and taken over recess. I'd call Veronica Grace Princess Bossy-Pants if I were allowed to call people names.

But I'm not.

So I won't.

Even though Veronica Grace is leaning over into my space and wrinkling her nose at my handwriting paper. "You make your cursive *E*s funny."

She holds up her paper. Her cursive *E* is loopy and swirly like it's supposed to be. Mine looks like a dog's been chewing on it, even though I really took my time. That is so not fair.

"All right, class. Listen up!" Mrs. Aloi shakes her maracas. "It's time for the most exciting part of our day. Marty, please collect everyone's papers, and then I'll have a big announcement."

I collect the papers super fast and hurry back to my seat to wait for Mrs. Aloi's big announcement. It must be huge news if it's going to be the most exciting part of our day.

"It's just about time for recess, but I know you've all been waiting to hear what the third-grade play will be," she says. "It's coming up in three weeks, so we'll be very busy getting ready. We will be practicing every day. This year, we've decided to perform our own version of an old fairy tale called *The Frog Prince.*"

"Is there dancing?" asks Kimmy Butler.

"Do we *have* to be in it?" asks Rupert Wingfield.

"Can I be the princess?" asks Veronica Grace Smithers.

"Can I, too?" asks Isabel Pike.

"Do we get to build props and stuff?" asks Alex Farley.

"Can I be the king?" asks Rasheena Wells.

"Can I do sound effects?" asks Jimmy Lawson. "I can burp so it sounds like a ribbit."

Mrs. Aloi shakes her maracas again. She says it's to remind us to listen, but I think she just likes shaking them. "We'll talk about all of that after recess. For now, just get thinking about kings and queens and castles, and get ready to have some out-of-your-seat fun."

I line up for recess, all excited. Out of my seat is my favorite place to be. Then I remember Mrs. Kramer's promise about third grade and that teachers have weird ideas about what's fun.

FIND OUT WHAT HAPPENS NEXT IN:

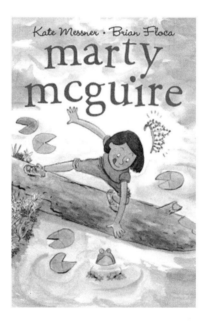